bruary 1998

ANN MAJOR

CHILDREN OF DESTINY
When Passion and Fate Intertwine...

SECRET CHILD

Although everyone told Jack West that his wife,
Chantal—the woman who'd betrayed him and sent
him to prison for a crime he didn't commit—had
died, Jack knew she'd merely transformed herself
into supermodel Mischief Jones. But when he
finally captured the woman he'd been hunting,
she denied everything. Who was she really—
an angel or a cunningly brilliant counterfeit?"

"Want it all? Read Ann Major."
—Nora Roberts, *New York Times*
bestselling author

Don't miss this compelling story
available at your favorite retail outlet.
Only from Silhouette books.

Silhouette®

As seen on TV!
Free Gift Offer

With a Free Gift proof-of-purchase from any Silhouette® book,
you can receive a beautiful cubic zirconia pendant.

This gorgeous marquise-shaped stone is a genuine cubic
zirconia—accented by an 18" gold tone necklace.
(Approximate retail value $19.95)

Send for yours today...
compliments of *Silhouette*®

To receive your free gift, a cubic zirconia pendant, send us one original proof-of-
purchase, photocopies not accepted, from the back of any Silhouette Romance™,
Silhouette Desire®, Silhouette Special Edition®, Silhouette Intimate Moments®
or Silhouette Yours Truly™ title available at your favorite retail outlet, together with
the Free Gift Certificate, plus a check or money order for $1.65 U.S./$2.15 CAN. (do
not send cash) to cover postage and handling, payable to Silhouette Free Gift Offer.
We will send you the specified gift. Allow 6 to 8 weeks for delivery. Offer good until
December 31, 1997, or while quantities last. Offer valid in the U.S. and Canada only.

Free Gift Certificate

Name: _____

Address: _____

City: _____ State/Province: _____ Zip/Postal Code: _____

Mail this certificate, one proof-of-purchase and a check or money order for postage
and handling to: SILHOUETTE FREE GIFT OFFER 1997. In the U.S.: 3010 Walden
Avenue, P.O. Box 9077, Buffalo NY 14269-9077. In Canada: P.O. Box 613, Fort Erie,
Ontario L2Z 5X3.

FREE GIFT OFFER   084-KFD
ONE PROOF-OF-PURCHASE
To collect your fabulous FREE GIFT, a cubic zirconia pendant, you must include this
original proof-of-purchase for each gift with the properly completed Free Gift Certificate.

084-KFDR

CHRISTINE FLYNN

Continues the twelve-book series—36 HOURS—in December 1997 with Book Six

FATHER AND CHILD REUNION

Eve Stuart was back, and Rio Redtree couldn't ignore the fact that her daughter bore his Native American features. So, Eve had broken his heart *and* kept him from his child! But this was no time for grudges, because his little girl and her mother, the woman he had never stopped—could never stop—loving, were in danger, and Rio would stop at nothing to protect *his* family.

For Rio and Eve and *all* the residents of Grand Springs, Colorado, the storm-induced blackout was just the beginning of 36 Hours that changed *everything!* You won't want to miss a single book.

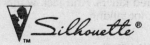

Desire Crystal Sweepstakes
Official Rules—No Purchase Necessary

To enter, complete an Official Entry Form or 3" x 5" card by hand printing the words "Desire Crystal Sweepstakes," your name and address thereon and mailing it to: in the U.S., Desire Crystal Sweepstakes, P.O. Box 9076, Buffalo, NY 14269-9076; in Canada, Desire Crystal Sweepstakes, P.O. Box 637, Fort Erie, Ontario L2A 5X3. Limit: one entry per envelope, one prize to an individual, family or organization. Entries must be sent via first-class mail and be received no later than 12/31/97. No responsibility is assumed for lost, late, misdirected or nondelivered mail.

Winners will be selected in random drawings (to be conducted no later than 1/31/98) from among all eligible entries received by D. L. Blair, Inc., an independent judging organization whose decisions are final. The prizes and their approximate values are: Grand Prize—a Mikasa Crystal Vase ($140 U.S.); 4 Second Prizes—a set of 4 Mikasa Crystal Champagne Flutes ($50 U.S. each set).

Sweepstakes offer is open only to residents of the U.S. (except Puerto Rico) and Canada who are 18 years of age or older, except employees and immediate family members of Harlequin Enterprises, Ltd., their affiliates, subsidiaries and all other agencies, entities and persons connected with the use, marketing or conduct of this sweepstakes. All applicable laws and regulations apply. Offer void wherever prohibited by law. Taxes and/or duties on prizes are the sole responsibility of the winners. Any litigation within the province of Quebec respecting the conduct and awarding of a prize in this sweepstakes may be submitted to the Régie des alcools, des courses et des jeux. All prizes will be awarded; winners will be notified by mail. No substitution for prizes is permitted. Odds of winning are dependent upon the number of eligible entries received.

Any prize or prize notification returned as undeliverable may result in the awarding of that prize to an alternative winner. By acceptance of their prize, winners consent to use of their names, photographs or likenesses for purposes of advertising, trade and promotion on behalf of Harlequin Enterprises, Ltd., without further compensation unless prohibited by law. In order to win a prize, residents of Canada will be required to correctly answer a time-limited, arithmetical skill-testing question administered by mail.

For a list of winners (available after January 31, 1998), send a separate stamped, self-addressed envelope to: Desire Crystal Sweepstakes 5309 Winners, P.O. Box 4200, Blair, NE 68009-4200, U.S.A.

Sweepstakes sponsored by Harlequin Enterprises Ltd., P.O. Box 9042, Buffalo, NY 14269-9042.

**Help us celebrate
15 years of unforgettable
romance with**

▼ SILHOUETTE®

Desire

You could win a genuine lead crystal vase, or
one of 4 sets of 4 crystal champagne flutes!
Every prize is made of hand-blown, hand-cut
crystal, with each process handled by master
craftsmen. We're making these fantastic gifts
available to be won by you, just for helping us
celebrate 15 years of the best romance reading
around!

DESIRE CRYSTAL SWEEPSTAKES
OFFICIAL ENTRY FORM

To enter, complete an Official Entry Form or 3" x 5"
card by hand printing the words "Desire Crystal
Sweepstakes," your name and address thereon and
mailing it to: in the U.S., Desire Crystal Sweepstakes,
P.O. Box 9076, Buffalo, NY 14269-9076; in Canada,
Desire Crystal Sweepstakes, P.O. Box 637, Fort Erie,
Ontario L2A 5X3. Limit: one entry per envelope, one
prize to an individual, family or organization. Entries
must be sent via first-class mail and be received no later
than 12/31/97. No responsibility is assumed for lost,
late, misdirected or nondelivered mail.

DESIRE CRYSTAL SWEEPSTAKES
OFFICIAL ENTRY FORM

Name: _____

Address: _____

City: _____

State/Prov.: _____ Zip/Postal Code: _____

KFO

15YRENTRY

Take 4 bestselling love stories FREE

Plus get a FREE surprise gift!

''All right, how about my family catching us in bed together?'' He bit back a groan at the memory of her smooth skin beneath his hands. For a solid week those memories had taunted him, tortured him. He remembered all too clearly her hushed whimpers. Her moans of pleasure and the tight hot feel of her body convulsing around his.

He felt a hardening in his groin, and he shifted position to lean against the doorjamb. It didn't help.

''Embarrassing,'' she said, tipping her head back to see him, ''but hardly earth-shattering.''

''Dammit, Casey!'' he snapped. ''What the hell difference does it make why I asked you to marry me? I did, you said yes and now we're married. Period.''

''It makes a difference, Jake.'' She unfolded her arms and stepped close to him. ''Just like the reason you came to save me from my parents' interrogation makes a difference.''

He wasn't sure why he had done that. He'd simply seen her alone, facing down two of the most intimidating people he'd ever known, and gone to help. Protective instincts were just that. Instincts.

''You looked like you could use a friend,'' was all he said.

''And you volunteered.''

''I *am* your husband.''

''So you are.'' She nodded absently, more to herself than to him. Then she ran her hands up his arms to encircle his neck.

''Casey.'' He stiffened under her touch, summon-

ing up every last ounce of control he could manage
to keep from grabbing her and holding her close.

"Jake," she said, and rose on her toes. Stopping
when her mouth was just a breath away from his, she
asked, "Aren't you curious about why I agreed to
marry you?"

"No." Yes, he thought, but not enough to ask.
Aloud he said, "Probably for the same reasons I proposed."

"Nope." She brushed her lips across his with a
feather touch.

He sucked in a breath and a groan emitted from
deep inside him. He curled his hands into fists at his
sides.

"It's really simple," she went on, then paused for
another brief kiss. "I figured it out myself just this
afternoon."

Jake knew what was coming. Even before she said
it, he felt it and braced for the impact of words he
didn't want to hear.

"I love you, Jake. Always have." She kissed him
again. "Always will."

His hormones stopped sizzling. The flames of desire died as abruptly as if they'd been doused with
ice water. Jake stared at her. She sensed that something was wrong. He could see it in her eyes. Slowly
her arms slid from around his neck, and she took a
single step back.

"Jake?"

"You love me?"

"Yeah."

She didn't sound very pleased about that anymore. Some consolation, he told himself.

"And a week ago," Jake reminded her, "you were going to marry somebody else. Did you 'love' him, too?"

"No."

"But you would have married him, anyway?"

"I like to think I would have said, 'I don't', but we'll never know, will we?"

"We sure won't." He pushed away from the door-jamb and inhaled sharply, ignoring the scent of her perfume as it invaded his lungs. Dammit, he wouldn't allow himself to feel for another woman. To depend on her. They tossed the word "love" around like it was a Frisbee. And the minute a man started to believe it, he was a goner.

Well, not Jake Parrish.

Not again.

If that meant this would be the first platonic marriage on record, then so be it. He'd hoped to reach a compromise of sorts between them. He'd hoped he and Casey could be friends—and lovers. After all, they'd already proved to be mutually satisfying bed partners.

His brain laughed at the weak description of what had happened between them less than a week ago.

But if she insisted on dragging *love* into this mess, he couldn't risk sharing her bed. As much as he wanted to, he wouldn't make love to her unless she understood that he couldn't love her. He wanted nothing more to do with love, thanks very much.

She sucked in a gulp of air and held it. His gaze

moved over her quickly, thoroughly. Despite the L-word hovering in the air between them, Jake felt a stirring in his groin again. He might think he knew exactly what he wanted. Apparently his body had other plans.

"Good night, Casey," he said abruptly, and left her while he still had the guts.

Little more than a week later nothing much had changed.

Casey sat at the kitchen table and stared blankly out the window. Her husband was out there somewhere with the foreman. Just as he'd been every day since the wedding, Jake had done everything he could to avoid spending time with her. Even at night, when the chores were finished and they might have had the chance to talk, he sequestered himself in the ranch office. He kept the door to that room, as well as the door to his heart, securely locked against her.

Thinking back, Casey knew the real trouble had started the moment she'd told her new husband she loved him. A wry smile lifted one corner of her mouth. Not exactly the words you would ordinarily expect to start a war.

She sighed and lifted her cup of coffee for a sip. She'd stopped keeping track of how much she'd already consumed that morning, telling herself to enjoy it while she could.

If what she suspected was true, she wouldn't be getting much caffeine for the next eight months or so.

The rich black brew slid down her throat, leaving

a trail of warmth for which she was grateful. She felt chilled. Inside and out. December had hit Simpson a few days ago, but even the recurring snow flurries couldn't hold a candle to the icy atmosphere inside the Parrish house.

She'd thought he might be surprised to hear her declaration of love. After all, even she had been taken aback momentarily when the realization struck her. But never had she expected Jake to turn into a tall dark handsome *stone*.

The phone rang and she scowled at it. Infuriating to be interrupted in the middle of a perfectly good pity party.

She snatched the receiver off the hook before it could ring again and snapped, "Hello?"

"Well, hi to you, too," Annie answered, and then had the nerve to chuckle.

"Sorry," Casey said. "I'm not myself today."

"Yeah, I remember how miserable *I* felt this early on."

"Annie…" She never should have said anything. Not even to her best friend. Not until she was sure. And certainly not until she'd talked to Jake.

"So have you done the test yet?"

"No."

"Well, why not? What are you waiting for? A burning bush? A tongue of flame perhaps?"

Casey frowned at the telephone. "If the answer is positive, it'll just create more problems around here."

"Case," her friend said softly, "*not* doing the test won't change anything."

"I know, I know." She reached out and picked up the pink-and-white box she'd purchased at the pharmacy the day before. Gripping it tightly, she said with forced lightness, "Besides, I'm probably not. I mean, what are the odds? About a million to one?"

"About."

"It's not like I haven't been late a day or two before."

"True."

"I'm worried about nothing. Right?"

"Right."

"Liar."

"Coward."

"Okay," Casey said on a sigh, "I'll do the test."

"Now?"

"As soon as I hang up."

"'Bye."

There was a click and then the tuneless hum of the dial tone. Thoughtfully Casey hung up the phone and stared down at the package in her hand.

"The moment of truth," she muttered, and headed for the bathroom.

Jake walked into the kitchen and stopped.

No enticing aroma welcomed him.

His gaze shot around the room. No pots were huddled on the stove. No elegant tempting dessert sat on the marble countertop. Even the coffeepot was empty, though the burner had been left on.

He stepped inside, turned off the coffeemaker, then looked around the empty room as if waiting for Casey to magically appear. Where was she? For the first time in their short marriage, she wasn't cooking. Surprising how quickly you became used to something. And he'd grown accustomed to hearing the clatter of pots, Casey's slightly off-key yet enthusiastic singing and, especially, the food.

The woman was a Michelangelo of the kitchen. After their wedding, people in Simpson had talked of little else but the meal she'd prepared almost single-handedly. It was no wonder she'd received more than a dozen phone calls asking her—no, *begging* her—to cater small holiday parties.

He snatched his hat off, scratched his head and went into the darkened hall. There were no lights on. Not even in the great room, where falling snow was displayed through the window in Christmas-card perfection. Frowning, he kept moving. Something was wrong.

He snorted a choked laugh at that understatement. What was *right* about their marriage? There probably weren't many newlywed couples who not only didn't share a bed but hardly spoke to each other. His fault, he knew. Casey had tried. But every time he felt himself weakening, wanting to hold her, kiss her, he heard her voice again, saying those three words that were enough to douse even *his* desire.

I love you.

He frowned and hastened his steps. At the end of the hall his bedroom door—*Casey's* bedroom door—stood wide open. He peered into the dusky room, whispering her name. No answer. His chest tightened. What the hell was going on? His gaze shifted. Across the room a slash of light underlined the bottom of the bathroom door. Cautiously he walked toward it.

From inside, he heard her muttering to herself and immediately felt relief wash through him. At least she was all right. Lifting one hand, he tapped gently on the door.

"Jake?"

Relieved beyond words to hear her speaking to him, he said, "Yeah. It's me. Are you OK?"

"Oh, sure," she said, then sniffed. "In the pink."

He frowned slightly. Something in her voice told him there was a problem. He wanted to know what it was.

"Casey? Open up."

"Go away, Jake."

All right. Now he *had* to know what was going on. He tossed his hat onto the bed behind him and faced the closed door as he would any other enemy.

"Casey, I'm not going anywhere until you tell me what's wrong."

She laughed. A short choked laugh that sounded painful.

"Casey, damn it…" He laid one palm against the wood as if he could feel her through the barrier. Worry sputtered into life inside him.

"Oh…"

"Are you going to open the door, or do I take it off the hinges?"

She laughed shortly, and even through the closed door, he could tell there was no humor in it.

"Probably simpler just to turn the knob," she said at last. "It's not locked."

He shook his head, grabbed the knob and turned it. As the door opened, light poured out of the room, and it took a second or two for his eyes to adjust. He saw her sitting on the rim of the tub, staring down at the white plastic stick in her hands.

"Casey?"

"White, no. Pink, yes."

"What did you say?"

"White, no. Pink, yes."

She wouldn't look at him. Her gaze was fixed on that damned stick as if it meant life or death. Irritation simmered inside him. He crossed his arms over his chest and stood there, feet wide apart in a comfortable stance he would keep just as long as it took him to get some answers.

"Why pink, do you think?"

"Pink what?" He tore his gaze from her bent head and glanced around the room looking for clues. Obviously she wasn't going to tell him what was wrong. He would have to find out for himself. He hadn't been in the master bathroom since the wedding. When had she had time to set pots of poinsettias in the terra-cotta window box along the back of the tub?

He shook his head slightly and continued his inspection. It seemed a little strange to see feminine jars and lotions lined up in perfect formation on a countertop that used to hold only a tube of toothpaste and a bottle of aftershave. His gaze landed on an unfolded set of instructions laying half in the sink. Frowning, he reached for it at the same moment she spoke again.

"Since it's pink, do you suppose that means it's a girl?"

He froze, then slowly swiveled his head to look at her.

"No," she argued with herself. "Pink just means pregnant. It could be a boy."

Girl? Boy? His mouth went dry and his brain blanked out. Was she saying what he thought she was saying? No. Of course she wasn't. It was only the one time. What were the odds?

She lifted her head and met his gaze through wide teary eyes, and he knew that odds or not, it was true.

"Congratulations, Jake. We're pregnant." She sucked in a breath, tightened her grip on that stick and squared her shoulders as if expecting a fight.

Pregnant. Uneasiness warred with pleasure and quickly lost. Delight trounced worry in a flat half second. Happiness battled viciously with anxiety and was clearly the winner.

Moments passed. Two or three heartbeats at most. But in that brief time, he saw at least a dozen different emotions flash across her features. Everything from dismay to joy to a fierce protectiveness glimmered in her watery green eyes.

He dropped to one knee in front of her, and the cold of the tile seeped through his denim jeans. Absently he told himself to have a carpet installed. He didn't want Casey getting sick—or worse, slipping and falling on wet tile.

He took the plastic stick from her hand and barely glanced at the deep-pink test square. Instead, he folded his hands around hers and felt a twinge of guilt at the icy feel of her skin.

"I'm not sorry, Jake," she said softly. "I know you don't want this baby, but I do. And I'll love it enough for both of us."

"You're wrong, Casey."

She blinked at him, clearly surprised. He couldn't really blame her—he felt a little stunned himself. But he would get over it. The important thing to remember here was that baby hadn't made itself. And whatever else happened between him and Casey, his child wasn't going to suffer for it.

"It's *our* baby," he said firmly, willing her to believe him. "*We're* going to have a baby. In fact, this is the best Christmas present I've ever received." He moved and sat down beside her on the edge of the tub. Draping one arm around her shoulders, he pulled her against him. "Whatever this marriage started out like, we just became a family."

Eight

A baby.

Three weeks ago he'd been blissfully contentedly single. Now he was an expectant father and married to a woman he hadn't seen in years. Jake's gaze lifted heavenward. Somebody up there had a very interesting sense of humor.

Casey straightened and shook her head, still staring at the test stick as if she couldn't quite believe this was happening.

"You know, staring at it won't make it change color."

She swung her gaze to him. "This is so weird."

"Being pregnant?"

"Not just that." She paused. "Although that is definitely the weirdest part. It's this whole situation, Jake."

He let his arm slip from her shoulder as he scooted closer to her on the tub's edge.

"Three weeks ago everything was different," she said.

Jake scowled, despite the fact that he'd been thinking the same thing only a minute ago.

"I was supposed to marry Steven, for heaven's sake." Casey let her gaze drop back down to the stick she held.

Fortunately she didn't see him flinch at her words. It still rankled him that she'd been able to switch gears so quickly when it came to choosing husbands.

"But then," she went on, more to herself than to him, "if I *had* married Steven, none of this would be happening."

True enough, but hardly relevant. She hadn't married Steven. Everything *had* happened, and they'd damn well better start dealing with it.

She rubbed the tip of one finger across the dark pink test square. "I don't think Steven wanted children."

That caught his attention. "Don't you *know?*"

Casey shook her head. "We didn't really talk much." She shot him a quick look. "I guess that makes me sound even worse, doesn't it? I mean that I was willing to marry a man I didn't even talk to."

"Hell, Casey, I don't know." And he didn't. She didn't strike him as the type of woman to be so cavalier with her affections. But then, what did he know about women? He'd married Linda.

"I don't even know how our engagement happened."

"What?"

"It's true. Sometimes I try to remember exactly when Steven proposed..."

It bothered him more than he wanted to admit that she'd been thinking about her ex-fiancé while married to *him*.

"But I don't think he ever really did. We both just drifted into this. Our parents were all for it, naturally."

Jake hadn't been too fond of Steven to begin with. Knowing that Casey's parents approved of the man made him even more disagreeable to Jake.

Abruptly deciding he'd heard quite enough about the runaway bridegroom, he pushed himself up from the edge of the tub and held one hand out to his wife.

"Enough about Steven, Casey."

She looked up at him, but didn't take the hand he offered.

"*We're* married now. *We* have a baby on the way."

"There's definitely a baby coming, Jake," she countered. "But as for being married, all we shared was a short ceremony."

"What?" Feeling a little foolish about his extended hand, which she refused to take, Jake let it fall to his side. "What are you talking about?"

She stood up and faced him. Granted, she had to tip her head back to do it, but somehow she managed to look intimidating, anyway.

"I'm talking about us. You. Me."

"You're not making sense."

"No, this marriage doesn't make sense."

He inhaled slowly, deeply. He'd been working diligently for the past two weeks. He'd kept his distance. He'd lain awake at night knowing she was lying in a bed only a few doors down the hall from him. He'd become accustomed to walking with his legs slightly bowed to accommodate a groin that was continually hard and aching.

And he'd suffered all of it for her sake. Didn't she understand what it cost him to keep his distance from her? Couldn't she tell how little sleep he was getting by the shadows under his eyes? Should he tell her how he lay awake at nights thinking about her? Remembering the feel, the scent, the taste of her?

"If we're married," she went on, oblivious to the tightening of his features, "don't you think we should at least *pretend* to be a real couple?"

"We don't have to pretend. We *are* a real couple. Harry married us. You were there."

"We're not a couple, Jake. We're two people living in the same house. We're housemates."

He rubbed one hand across his face and struggled to draw air into his lungs. "Casey, I told you, I think we both need time to adjust to this."

"If you regret marrying me, Jake," she said calmly, "just say so. I'll have my father arrange a divorce. There's nothing he'd like better."

His gaze snapped to hers. Anger bubbled up inside him. He didn't care if it was reasonable or not. That she could talk so easily about a divorce bothered him more than he could say.

"There's no divorce coming, Casey." He gritted his teeth and went on, squeezing his voice past a tight throat. "Get used to it. I'm not going through that again. And dammit, I'm not going to let *my* child go through it."

Casey felt a chill from his words and expression, as she would have from a brisk northern wind. His eyes narrowed and she sensed the tension in him. She hadn't *meant* it. She didn't want a divorce. She wanted a husband. The husband she loved.

Apparently, though, she was going about it in all the wrong ways. Fine. Swallowing back her impatience, she said, "You're right. There is no divorce for us, Jake. I don't want that, either."

He seemed to relax a little, so she plunged ahead.

"But I want more than a housemate, too." She waited for him to argue with her. But he didn't say anything, so she went on, "I want someone to talk to. To laugh with. To plan with."

He was softening. She could see it in his eyes.

"To love," she added, and almost groaned as she saw tension arc back into his body.

"Let's leave love out of this, all right?"

"How do you leave love out of a marriage?"

He gave her a wry smile. "Trust me. It's easier to leave it out than to try to keep it in."

Disappointment quivered through her. Jake always had been stubborn. A less stubborn man would have given in to her clumsy seduction attempt five years before and saved both of them from missed chances at happiness. Casey frowned at him, studying the sharp planes of his face as she would a text written in an unfamiliar language.

Because of his sense of honor, his conscience, they

had both lost the past five years. Casey had no doubt that if he hadn't turned her away that long-ago night, they would have known the magic that sparked between them for what it was. They would have stayed together. And maybe this child that was coming now would have been their second. Or third.

"Now come on," he said, and snatched up her hand. "Let's get you something to eat."

As they moved through the dark house headed for the kitchen, Jake turned on the lights they passed. Soon the big ranch house was well lit, warm and welcoming.

It struck her then exactly how she would have to go about winning her husband. One light at a time, until finally all the shadows were chased from his soul.

"See?" Jake straightened the aerial map lying on his desk and pointed to a section of land that had been highlighted in bright red ink.

Casey leaned over his shoulder, and he forced himself to take slow shallow breaths. Just the scent of her was enough to drive him insane. Having the length of her soft shining hair streaming alongside his cheek was especially dangerous. He knew what her hair smelled like. Roses and promises. If he took a deep breath, dragging that scent into him, there was no way he would be able to keep a grip on his rising tide of desire.

"Who drew the red line around it?" she asked, and tilted her head to look at him.

"Me." Deliberately he shifted his gaze from hers.

Staring into emerald green eyes was not the way to maintain an even keel. "I've wanted that land for years. Outlined it to help me focus on it."

"Ah."

The knowing tone in her voice made him turn to look at her again, despite his better judgment. For the past few days, ever since the night they'd discovered her pregnancy, he'd made a concerted effort to be a better husband. These days, after dinner, they sat together in the great room. They watched movies, idiotic television shows that he couldn't concentrate on with her sitting beside him, and they talked about his plans for the ranch or the catering jobs she'd been offered. He listened to her talk excitedly of their first Christmas together and tried to share her eagerness.

They did everything together but share a bedroom. It didn't matter that all he thought about these days was being with her. Holding her. Sliding into her warmth and burying himself inside her. Danger lay down that path. That was a risk he still couldn't bring himself to take. Not yet.

But there was something else to consider, too. He had no intention of being celibate for the rest of his life. So what he had to do was give himself enough time to distance himself emotionally from Casey before starting in on the physical side of their marriage. Once he'd accomplished that, everything would go much more smoothly.

She was watching him.

He pushed his thoughts aside and reached back to pick up the threads of their conversation.

"What do you mean, ah?"

"Nothing." She lifted one shoulder in an elegant shrug. "It's just that I had no idea you were interested in positive visualization."

"Positive what?"

"Visualization." Casey straightened and took a step to one side. Jake drew his first easy breath since they'd entered his office.

"I don't know what you're talking about," he said. "All I did was draw a line around something I wanted."

"Exactly. Positive visualization means that you focus your energies on the object of your desire and harness the energies of the universe to help you get it."

He laughed. He couldn't help it. She looked so damned serious. As if telling the universe was all you needed to do to solve your problems. Shaking his head, he felt his laughter slowly drain away as he noticed she wasn't laughing with him.

"Several books have been written on the subject, you know."

"Books have been written on UFOs, too."

Her lips twitched. "Hardly the same thing."

"Right." He nodded sagely. "Different universes."

"Although," Casey said thoughtfully, "those books are very interesting. I believe my favorite is the one about gods in chariots."

Jake snorted and rolled his eyes.

"Fine," she said as she turned for the door. "All I'm saying is that you focused your energies and the universe's, and you got what you wanted."

"Sure," Jake countered, getting to his feet and following her. "As soon as I came up with the cash Don wanted for the land."

"Exactly."

He laughed again. Odd, but he didn't remember laughing so much in years as he had the past few days with Casey. "What's *that* mean?"

She settled onto her end of the long couch in the main room and waited for him to sit down beside her before answering. "You were able to find the money once the universe had obliged you by arranging everything else."

Jake leaned his head back against the cushions and stared up at the ceiling. "You're amazing."

"Thank you."

He wasn't prepared. He hadn't heard a thing. When at least thirty pounds of snuffling drooling fur landed on his stomach, his breath whooshed out of him.

"Hello, baby," Casey crooned, and laughed as the dog wriggled ecstatically on Jake's stomach.

"Get off, you flea-bitten mangy excuse for a dog!"

The big puppy's head drooped and both ears flopped down to rest against its cheeks.

"Jake, you hurt his feelings."

If the dog had landed an inch or two lower on his abdomen, it would have hurt something a tad more precious to Jake than his feelings. Looking into sad brown eyes, though, he did feel almost guilty for shouting.

Almost.

"It's all right, Stumbles," Casey soothed. "Come over here, and never mind Daddy."

Jake's eyes widened. "I am *not* that dog's daddy."

She wasn't paying any attention to him. But then, neither was the dog. For a moment he watched as his wife cuddled and stroked the ugliest animal he'd ever seen.

Gray and black hair stood out in odd tufts over its forehead and legs. Its ears were lopsided, giving the impression that the dog's head was continually cocked, and it had the biggest feet Jake had ever seen on anything smaller than an elephant. He shuddered to even think about how big that hound was going to get.

He still wasn't sure exactly how they'd come to own a dog. He wasn't entirely certain that Casey knew, either. Stumbles, so christened because he tripped over his own feet, had simply appeared one evening at dinnertime and hadn't left.

Yet.

Casey had immediately dubbed the puppy their "Christmas visitor" and calmly informed Jake that it would bring terrible luck down on them if they were to turn him away.

"He's not ugly," she said quietly.

Jake's gaze shot to hers. "How'd you know that's what I was thinking?"

"It wasn't hard. You say it often enough." Stumbles scooted himself around until he lay in the small space separating Casey and Jake on the couch. Laying his head on his mistress's thigh, he closed his eyes and promptly began to snore.

Jake's eyebrows lifted as he took in the animal's position. A hell of a note—envying a disreputable hound.

"I always wanted a dog," she whispered.

Jake watched her fingertips trace lightly over Stumbles's ragged fur. Her voice sounded so wistful his insides twisted, bringing a pain he didn't want to feel. Or acknowledge. He could just imagine what her parents' reaction to a dog like Stumbles would have been. They would have called the pound immediately of course. And no one visiting the shelter to adopt a cute puppy would have given Stumbles a glance.

Jake frowned and looked at the happily snoring mutt. If not for Casey, Stumbles would no doubt have ended up walking that long last mile.

Instantly memories of Casey as a teenager raced through his mind. He recalled how much she'd loved the animals on the ranch. From the barn cats to the horses, she'd never been able to get enough. No doubt, the Oakeses' idea of a family pet was the buffalo on one side of a nickel.

It must have been hard for someone as loving and caring as Casey to grow up in such a cold home.

He pushed that notion aside and said gruffly, "Well, if he's going to stay, we'd better get him to the vet for his shots."

Casey grinned and Jake felt oddly rewarded.

"He'll need a collar, too," she said. "And tags. We wouldn't want anyone to steal him."

Jake laughed and Stumbles snorted, clearly disturbed by the racket. There wasn't a chance in hell

that anyone but Casey would steal the ugly Stumbles.
But if she wanted to get the dog collared and tagged,
that was what they would do.

He was just being nice, he told himself. After all,
she was the mother of his child.

It was the least he could do.

A few days later Casey stood in the modern
well-equipped ranch kitchen and surveyed her handi-
work. Every muscle in her body ached. She'd been
up half the night completing this order, but it was
worth it.

So many things had changed in such a short
amount of time. Married, pregnant and, apparently,
a new and flourishing career.

"Who would have thought it, Stumbles?" she
murmured to the dog lying beneath the kitchen table.

His tail thumped against the floor and a low plead-
ing whine issued from his throat.

"Not a chance," she said on a laugh. "These
goodies are not for you."

Sorrowfully the dog laid his head down on his
paws and watched her as she walked the length of
the room, inspecting everything.

She looked at the carefully arranged trays laid out
on the countertops and went over the list in her hand
for the third time.

"Napoleons, check. Crème brûlées, check. Eclairs,
check." Each and every order received a final inspection. "Ladyfingers, check. Petits fours, check.
And cookies..." Dozens of them—stars, angels, san-
tas—each dusted with crushed silver dragées and

looking fit for a fairy feast. When she reached the end of the counter, she sighed and nodded to herself.

Finished. And if she did say so herself, a nice job, too.

This was by far the most important catering job she'd been offered since the wedding. The Ladies Guild of Greater Simpson's annual Christmas fundraiser could be the start of something wonderful for her. Or, a little voice inside taunted, a fiery crash into disaster.

"Ready?"

She spun around to see Jake, standing in the doorway. Dressed in jeans, a worn flannel shirt, with the sleeves rolled up past his elbows, he took her breath away. He leaned against the doorjamb, arms folded over his chest, his blue eyes fixed on her in a way that made her heart race and her mouth go dry.

Yet even as she watched him, that look faded from his eyes and was replaced by a detached friendly concern. Casey felt a familiar swell of disappointment rise in her. It didn't seem to matter that they were getting along better and better. It didn't seem to count with him that they had fun together. They still weren't sharing a bedroom. He still insisted on holding himself back from her. Not just his body.

His heart.

"Casey?"

"Hmm?" She shook her head. "Sorry. Daydreaming, I guess."

He nodded and pushed away from the doorway. Walking toward her, he said, "So, are you ready to go?"

"Jake, you don't have to take me to town. I can drive the truck myself."

"No trouble. Besides, I don't want you lifting all these trays in and out of the truck bed."

She inhaled deeply and nodded.

"You look tired," he said, and his husky voice sent awareness skittering through her.

She swallowed back her reaction and said, "I am. The order took most of the night."

"It's not good for you," he told her, "staying up that late. Working this hard." His gaze swept over her quickly, thoroughly. "You're pregnant, Casey. You need to get rest."

"I'm fine, Jake."

He didn't look convinced.

"When's your doctor's appointment?"

"This afternoon. At three."

"You sure the doctor won't mind if I'm there, too, will she?"

She smiled at him. "She said that all fathers are welcome—as long as they behave."

"Good." He nodded and picked up the flattened pastry boxes. As he folded one of them into shape, he said, "I want to ask her about all this catering stuff you're doing. Don't want you injuring yourself or the baby."

"Jake..."

"It won't hurt to ask."

She sighed and changed the subject. "I thought I'd visit with Annie until it was time to go to the doctor's office."

"OK," he said, then picked up a tray of éclairs

and slid it into the waiting box. "I've got some business in town, so we can deliver your goodies first, then drop you off at the hairdresser. I'll pick you up when it's time."

She knew it would be pointless to argue. She'd tried to tell him there was no need for him to accompany her to the doctor. He hadn't listened then, so there was no reason to suppose he would listen now.

Whatever else she could say about him, he certainly seemed determined to be a good father.

That was a start.

Wasn't it?

Nine

"**I** think I'm losing my mind."

Frank Parrish laughed at his son's serious tone and waved him to a chair. "You're not losing your mind, Jake. You're just spending too much time arguing with your common sense, instead of listening to it."

Jake turned away from the window and the view of Simpson City Park. Several men were setting up the town Christmas tree. He was *not* in a holiday frame of mind. Studying his father, seated in a worn but comfortable easy chair, he asked, "What's that supposed to mean?"

"I think you know what it means, and that's what's got you so scared."

"Scared?" He barked a laugh and shook his head. "I'm certainly not scared, Dad."

"Don't know what else you'd call it, then," Frank

said. "You've got a real nice wife—pretty, too. A baby on the way, a good ranch, big house and all the land you've ever wanted. If you're not scared, why aren't you happy?"

It did sound ridiculous when put like that. But dammit, he'd had most of those things before, too. And it hadn't changed anything. Linda had still walked out. Leaving him reeling.

How could he risk having Casey do the same thing?

"She's not Linda," his father said softly.

"I never said she was."

"You didn't have to say it. It's in your eyes every day."

"What?"

"Every day, you're waiting for the ax to fall. You keep looking out for the thunderclouds, you never notice the sunshine."

"And if I'm not watching for the storm, I get caught up in it. Then what?"

"You get wet."

Jake laughed shortly.

"Then you dry off again and start over."

"No, thanks." If the storm came this time, Jake knew it would be far worse than the drizzle he had faced at Linda's hands. He was sure of it, because he cared far more for Casey than he had ever thought possible.

Every day spent with her was a good day. Listening to her, hearing her move around the once-silent house with that damned dog at her heels, was like music to him. He hadn't even known how lonely he really was until Casey had come.

But if he let himself care for her, if he told her he loved her, only to lose her, the pain would kill him.

"It's your decision of course."

"What is?" Jake's gaze locked with his father's.

"To let yourself enjoy the second chance you've been given."

Jake stiffened and shook his head.

"Or," Frank went on, "to turn your back on it and live the half life you've been living for the past few years."

Some choice.

Lonely?

Or dead inside because he took a chance?

"So, how you feeling these days, pregnant lady?"

Casey grinned at Annie. "Great." The grin slipped a bit. "Aren't I supposed to be feeling terrible? Do you think something's wrong?"

"I think everything's fine and you worry too much." Annie pulled a wide-toothed comb through her customer's wet iron gray hair. "You should be like Mrs. Dieter here. Don't worry about a thing." She raised her voice to a near shout. "Isn't that right, Mrs. Dieter?"

"Who's gonna fight?" the old lady yelled.

Casey laughed quietly, briefly met Annie's amused gaze, then looked around. The sharp distinctive odor of permanent solution hung in the air of the tiny beauty shop. Annie was the owner and sole employee, so her customers always had to wait, but as Annie liked to tell them, she was worth it.

Casey wandered around the small room, admiring pots of flowers and hanging plants that made the waiting area look like a rain forest. Gold and silver stars were sprinkled amid the greenery, and life-size posters of both Santa Claus and Frosty the Snowman were hung on the walls. Multicolored lights twinkled around the windowframe, and Christmas carols drifted quietly from a tape player in the corner.

A floor-to-ceiling bookshelf along one wall was lined with paperbacks, and the latest magazines and mail-order catalogs lay scattered across a low table set in the middle of four overstuffed chairs.

Since she was waiting to go to lunch with Annie, Casey sat down in one of those chairs, snatched up a catalog and made herself comfortable.

"I won't be much longer," Annie said. "Mrs. Dieter was an emergency cut. Her grandson's coming to take her out on the town." Annie's voice rose in volume again. "Joe's quite the dancer."

"How can I answer you if I can't hear your question?" The old lady sniffed and closed her eyes, apparently deciding to catch a quick nap in the chair.

With a smile Annie glanced at Casey and asked, "So how's my big brother taking the news of impending fatherhood?"

"I think he's pleased about the whole thing." Actually she wasn't sure, but she certainly heard Jake muttering, "A *baby*," to himself often enough to know he was thinking about it.

"Well, why shouldn't he be?"

Indeed. Casey only wished he was half as pleased about being a husband. Oh, things had definitely improved between them in the short time since she'd done the pregnancy test. They actually *talked* in the evenings. Jake was always solicitous, offering to make her tea, bring her a pillow. He was sort of the 1950s movie version of a soon-to-be father. The only thing he hadn't done was boil water.

But they still slept in separate rooms, and any time the conversation took a turn to the personal, he took a turn to the door. Emotionally speaking of course.

"How's everything…else going?"

Casey glanced up from the catalog. "The same," she said, and hated the defeated note in her voice. But really, what more could she do? She'd tried seducing him five years before. Apparently she wasn't very good at it.

Besides, how did you go about seducing your husband?

"Jake always was too stubborn for his own good. It's amazing you even *got* pregnant." Annie tugged at a stubborn knot, and the old woman opened her eyes to glare at her in the mirror. "Sorry, Mrs. Dieter."

Casey folded the corner of a page down over a couple of items she wanted to order, then asked, "You think one of these magazines of yours will have an article on how to get your husband back in bed?"

Annie opened her mouth, but Mrs. Dieter cut her off.

"Meet him at the door naked," she said sharply. "Worked on Mr. Dieter every time."

Casey looked at Annie.

Annie looked at Casey.

Then they both stared at the wizened old woman.

"For Christmas," Mrs. Dieter added, "I used to wear a big ol' red ribbon tied around my chest with a great big bow right in the middle of my boobies." She glanced down sadly at her pendulous breasts. "I had real perky boobies back then, too. Always brightened Mr. Dieter right up, seeing them."

A stunned silence stretched out in the room before the woman snapped, "You think I was *born* old?"

Annie laughed first, then bent down and kissed the woman's papery cheek. "Mrs. Dieter, today's hairstyle is on the house."

"You may call me Agnes."

As Annie and Agnes laughed together, Casey sank back into the cushions. Staring blankly out the window, she giggled and told herself that what was good for Mr. Dieter, might just be good for Mr. Parrish.

On the way from the snowy parking lot to the doctor's office, Casey and Jake passed four people who stopped to offer congratulations on their coming baby. As the last well-wisher moved off, Casey said, "Now how do you suppose everybody found out about the baby already?"

Jake took her hand and pulled her toward the shiny new medical building. "No supposing about it," he said wryly. "I told you that Emma with a phone in her hand could outdo supermarket tabloids."

"She's *good*," Casey muttered.

He glanced down at her and smiled. "Now aren't you glad we only told her and Uncle Harry yesterday? Think what she could have done if she'd had more than a week."

"It chills the blood." Casey shook her head and hurried to keep pace with Jake's long strides. Emma and Harry weren't the only people they'd waited to tell. She still had to break the news to her parents that they were going to have a grandchild. Talk about blood-chilling.

A few minutes later they were being ushered through the empty waiting room to the examining room. Casey stepped behind a dressing screen, took off her clothes and donned a ridiculously sheer open-in-the-back, pink cotton gown. When she climbed onto the table, she turned to Jake.

"You don't have to stay for this part, you know. You could just come in when the doctor's finished and ask any questions you might have."

He glanced at the cold steel stirrups, already up and waiting for her feet, then shifted his gaze back to her. "It's all right. If you don't mind, I'd rather stay."

She squeezed a laugh past her suddenly tight throat. "It's OK with me."

A moment later Dr. Dianna Hauck bustled into the room, her nurse right behind her, and grinned at them.

"So," the doctor began, "pregnant, huh?"

"That's what the test kit says."

The doctor shook her head and said wryly, "Those

blasted kits are putting me out of business." Glancing at Jake, she asked, "You staying?"

"If it's all right."

"OK by me, just keep out of the way." Dr. Hauck laughed, pulled up a stool and sank onto it. "That's what I'll be telling you when we're in the delivery room, so get used to it."

Jake inhaled sharply and one of the doctor's eyebrows lifted.

"OK, Casey, take the position." The nurse handed Dr. Hauck a pair of latex gloves and she snapped them on.

Jake took the woman at her word and moved to the head of the table. Casey reached back and took his hand. His fingers curled around hers. Her skin felt cold. Was she as nervous as he was?

What if the kit had been wrong? What if there was no baby? Would he be pleased? Or disappointed? He looked down into Casey's green eyes and saw his own anxieties staring back at him.

It was over in a matter of minutes.

"You can sit up now," the doctor said as she rose and walked to the sink, pulling off her gloves as she went. While she washed her hands, she looked over her shoulder at them. "My best guess is that in about eight months or so you'll be parents."

Jake released a breath he hadn't realized he'd been holding. A warm delightful feeling settled in his chest. That settled that. He was pleased about the baby.

Moving closer to Casey, he instinctively tightened

his grip on her hand and began asking all of the usual about-to-be-a-father questions.

The very next evening Casey turned the dimmer on the kitchen light switch until the room was softly lit. She raised the lid on the pot at the back of the stove, gave the contents a quick stir, then resettled the lid.

She looked around the room. Stumbles wasn't around, tucked into his blanket in Jake's office. The table was elegantly set. Counters and cooking island cleaned off. Fire burning in the hearth. Beef stew simmering. Freshly made éclairs waiting in the refrigerator.

Everything was ready.

Even her.

She smoothed her hair one last time as she heard Jake's Jeep pull into the yard. Tossing a quick glance out the curtained window, she saw him climb out of the Jeep and reach back inside for the tools he'd picked up at the hardware store.

Her stomach flipped over and she took a deep steadying breath. It was time to find out if Mrs. Dieter knew what she was talking about.

She glanced down at herself, sighed, then tugged at the wide red ribbon tied around her chest. The bow between her breasts was a little crooked, but she didn't think Jake would mind. She hoped he would be too busy doing something else to worry about the aesthetics.

She shivered in the somewhat cool room and told herself she should have stayed closer to the fireplace.

Naked but for the bright red bow, she was beginning to get downright cold. Not to mention just a tad uneasy.

Inhaling sharply, she tried not to think about what she might be setting herself up for. She groaned quietly at the humiliating images leaping to life in her mind. What if he walked in the door, took one look at her and *laughed?* Or worse yet, walked right past her and didn't even *notice* she was naked?

Won't happen, she told herself. She knew darn well he wanted her every bit as much as she did him.

The outside door opened, then shut again, and Casey tensed. If this little stunt didn't reach him, she wasn't sure what would. She struck a pose, hoping to look nonchalant, and waited.

Jake set the bag down on a table, then stopped in the mudroom long enough to shrug out of his coat, tug off his boots and toss them onto the newspaper spread out alongside the door. He sniffed the air, appreciating the delicious aroma drifting from the kitchen. A man could get used to this. It wasn't so long ago that he had come home from a long day to an empty house and a frozen microwave dinner.

But that was before Casey.

He slumped back against the wall and asked himself how he was going to keep living with his wife and not make love to her. It was harder every day to ignore her presence. To ignore the small but pleasant changes she'd made to the house. To his life.

How could he live with her and *not* fall in love with her?

Keep remembering Linda, he thought. Remember

what it had been like to find out she'd been lying about loving him. Remember the pain.

Nodding abruptly, he straightened and crossed to the sink on the opposite wall. He washed up quickly, then moved to the kitchen door. He stepped into the warm fragrant room and all rational thought dissolved.

"Merry Christmas, Jake."

He blinked, shook his head and blinked again as if expecting the apparition in front of him to disappear.

"Casey?"

His body tightened as his gaze swept over her. In the soft light her skin looked as pale and creamy as fine porcelain. The wide ribbon wrapped around her chest and across her erect nipples came together in a slightly askew bow in the valley between her breasts. The ends of the ribbon trailed across her abdomen, drawing his gaze down to the light brown triangle of curls at the juncture of her thighs. As he admired her, she shifted position and the ribbon swayed gently with her movement.

Mouth dry, heart pounding in his chest, Jake knew his valiant struggle was over. No more battling his instincts. No more distance between them. At some point he would have to find a way to live with this incredible—and surprising—woman without falling in love with her.

But not today.

"It's three weeks until Christmas," he said finally, and congratulated himself on getting his voice to work.

"Close enough." She shrugged and his breath caught as the ribbon across her breasts dipped a bit.

His gaze stroked across her body, slowly, hungrily. A Christmas package. Santa had never been *this* good to him before.

Minutes ticked by. He had to say something. But what?

"Dinner smells good." Brilliant.

"Beef stew."

He nodded and noticed the grip she had on the edge of the cooking island. Her knuckles were white. Nerves? Swinging his gaze back to hers, he asked, "What's for dessert?"

She cleared her throat, again shifted from foot to foot and glanced at the refrigerator. "Chocolate éclairs."

"I'd rather have you."

Her breath caught, the tension in her shoulders eased, and she released her death grip on the island. She took a hesitant step toward him and Jake wanted to kick himself. Had he done this to her? Made her so anxious? So unsure of herself? Yes, he had.

To protect himself. Something to be proud of, he thought with disgust. Whether they had planned this marriage or not, Casey was his *wife* and deserved better than she had gotten so far from him.

Starting now, this minute, he would give her everything he could give. And hopefully it would be enough to keep her from missing what he simply didn't have anymore.

"Jake?"

He smiled and watched the lines between her

finely arched brows disappear. "I don't believe I've ever been welcomed home so warmly."

"Welcome? Yes," she said, and grinned wryly. "Warm?" She shivered a bit. "Not really."

Goose bumps raced along her arms and legs. He went to her quickly and pulled her into his arms. Running his hands up and down her supple body, he whispered, "Maybe you should have waited to try this in the summer."

"I didn't want to wait," she said, and drew her head back to look at him. "Not anymore."

He lifted one hand to caress her cheek and groaned when she turned a kiss into his palm. "I'm glad you didn't wait."

"Me, too."

Glancing down at her ribbon-wrapped body, he gave her a half smile before asking, "Am I allowed to open my Christmas present this early?"

"You're allowed just about anything tonight," she said softly. She trembled again and his right hand began to stroke up and down her spine.

"Still cold?" he whispered.

Another tremor rocketed through her. "Not now."

"Good," he said just before he dipped his head to claim the kiss for which, he'd been hungering for days.

She leaned into him, liquid sensual heat, and Jake knew the moment his mouth came down on hers that no matter what else happened between them, he would never again keep himself from her. As long as she wanted him, he would be there.

Her lips parted his and his tongue thrust inside to

restake his claim on her. Caressing, exploring, he rediscovered her with all of the eagerness and excitement of their first night together.

He felt her hands slide up his arms to his shoulders. Felt her fingers spear through his hair. Her breath puffed against his cheek. His hands moved up and down her back in long smooth motions over skin that seemed as perfect, as sleek as the finest china.

Raising one hand, he cupped her breast and, through the satiny texture of the ribbon, rubbed his thumb across her hardened nipple until a low deep-throated moan escaped her. She arched against him and Jake held her tighter, closer.

Her hands slipped to the front of his shirt and beneath the soft flannel fabric to his chest. He shuddered at her touch, then pulled back from her only long enough to tug his shirt off and toss it to the floor.

She reached for him, but he caught her hands. His gaze moved over her slowly, admiringly. "When someone gives me a package, all neatly done up in ribbon, it's *my* present. Right?"

"Yeah..."

"And," he said as he reached for one dangling end of the ribbon, "you *did* say I was allowed *anything* tonight, didn't you?"

"Yeah, I guess so." She shivered a bit as he tugged on the ribbon.

The big bow came loose and fell to the floor at her feet in a whisper of sound. Jake smiled and both black eyebrows rose as he set his hands at her waist and lifted her to sit on the edge of the cooking island.

"What are you up to?" she asked.

"Why, Casey," he admonished, and took the few steps to the refrigerator, "don't you trust me?"

"Sure, but what..." Her voice faded as she watched him pull the chocolate éclairs out of the fridge.

He set the tray of pastries on the table, then picked up one éclair and walked back to her. Dipping his index finger into the luscious cream filling, he scooped out a generous dollop, held it toward her and said softly, "I'm having my dessert first."

Ten

The countertop under her bottom was cold, but the look in Jake's eyes made the blood in her veins sizzle.

She swallowed heavily and watched him come closer. When her knees brushed his bare chest, he stopped. Seated on the cooking island, she was at eye level with her husband, and she kept her gaze locked with his as he offered her the fingerful of heavy sweetened cream. The flavor exploded in her mouth, but when she reached for the éclair to offer some to him, Jake shook his head.

"I'll get my own," he said softly, then bent to taste first one of her breasts, then the other. Tenderly, delicately, his tongue stroked her nipples as if she were indeed a rare luscious dessert. Her fingers curled around the edge of the island and she held on tight as wave after wave of delight crashed through her.

Sharp dagger points of need began to stab at her center, making her ache with wanting him. A deep inner throbbing pulsed along with her heartbeat, and her breath came in ragged gasps. Arching into his wonderful mouth, she offered herself to him, hoping for, needing, more.

He chuckled gently and lifted his head. "*My* present," he reminded her with one quick kiss on her lips.

Ridiculous to suddenly feel...not *uneasy. Embarrassed?* This whole naked-in-the-kitchen thing had seemed like such a good idea at the time. She noted the gleam in his eye and experienced an answering tremor that shook her insides. The brief attack of awkwardness disappeared in a rush of something she could only describe as...intoxicating.

"Jake," she said, her voice just a touch playful, "nice men don't torture their wives."

"Ah," he countered with a wink, "but what wife wants her husband to be *nice?*"

"Me?"

"No, you don't, Casey," he assured her, and eased her back until she was lying down on the island, knees bent at the edge and her feet dangling. "You much prefer me *adventurous.*"

"Just how adventurous are we talking about here?" Nerves fluttered in her chest again. "Maybe I should warn you that I'm not normally the adventurous type."

"That's not what your ribbon said."

True. No way to argue that. But then, she admitted silently, she didn't really want to argue with whatever he had in mind. She'd waited long enough for this moment and damned if she wouldn't enjoy herself.

She lifted her head to watch him as he walked to the end of the island and positioned himself between her legs. She gasped when he dipped one finger into the éclair filling again and reached for her.

"Jake..."

"My present," he reminded her. "My dessert."

Then he touched the icy filling to her hottest flesh, and she jumped, startled at the sensation. "It's cold!"

"Not for long," he said, and his voice sounded thick, husky.

Casey shuddered. Through half-closed eyes, she watched him as he lowered his mouth to her center. As he covered her, she groaned and let her head drop back to the countertop.

His tongue smoothed through the cool thick cream, swirling it around her flesh, stroking it, tasting it. He lapped at her body with a slow deliberation that pushed Casey's nerve endings into a frenzy of need. Her legs parted farther, inviting him closer, deeper.

He drove her toward madness and taunted her with release. His mouth created fires of desperation, and his tongue introduced her to delights she hadn't dreamed existed.

With every intimate caress, he became more a part

of her. He touched more than her body. He touched
her heart. Her soul.

As much as her body hummed from his attentions,
her soul soared. This is what they were meant to be,
she thought dazedly. His touch reached beyond the
physical and eased her spirit.

Together.

Forever.

"Jake…" She felt it coming. Her body tightened
in expectation. Tingles of awareness brightened,
glowing inside her like a Fourth of July fireworks
display. Her breath caught. She reached for the prize
dangling just out of her grasp. She strained, aching
for the completion he offered her. Then a spectacular
bolt of pure pleasure rocketed through her. She stiffened and cried his name in a strangled voice.

A few moments later she lay limp on the counter
and felt him delicately washing away the last of the
sugared cream filling from her body. She jumped as
he brushed over the still-sensitive flesh. When he finally finished, she opened her eyes to look up at him.

Passion darkened his gaze, and though her climax
had only just passed, she felt desperate for him again.
To feel him atop her. Inside her. Joined to her as
deeply as he had been on that magical night that had
led to their marriage. She reached for him and cuddled close to his chest as he scooped her up and
carried her down the hallway to the master bedroom.

He laid her in the center of the mattress, tore off
the rest of his clothes and lay down beside her. His
hands moved over her roughly, hurriedly, as if he

had waited too long to touch her. As if he couldn't touch her enough.

Desperation rose in Jake and shattered inside his chest. Need like he'd never known before swamped him. His body ached for her. Casey's flesh beneath his hands became a song in his brain that repeated over and over. A tune he couldn't name and couldn't forget. A melody that had somehow, despite his efforts to prevent it, etched its way into his heart and become as much a part of his life as breathing.

She kissed him, opening her mouth to him, inviting his caress. She took his breath for her own and gave him hers. And when he couldn't bear to be separate from her another moment, she opened her body to him, welcoming him inside.

He groaned aloud as he pushed into her and felt her heat surround him, invade him. She locked her legs around his hips and held him tight within her until his world finally exploded, leaving only her warmth to shelter him.

A short time later they lay entwined on the bed, Casey's head pillowed on his chest. Jake ran one hand up and down her back, marveling at the softness of her skin and the incredible gift of having her in his life.

Even as he thought it, though, he turned from the realization that he was coming to care too much for her. He wouldn't let it happen again. He wouldn't allow himself to be such a fool for love that when it was over he was left with nothing.

She stirred against him, dropped a quick kiss on his chest and draped one arm across his body.

It felt good. Right.

And terrifying.

"Is dinner ruined?" He blurted the question in self-defense, to keep himself from wandering too far down a path he couldn't risk taking.

"You can think about food at a time like this?" she teased, and raised herself on one elbow to look at him.

"I don't have the strength to think of anything else." He flicked her a glance and smiled tiredly. "Not until I get something to eat."

"Then by all means," she countered, "let's feed you."

She rolled to one side and snatched up one of his T-shirts from a stack of fresh laundry. Holding it up in front of her, she asked, "Shall we dress for dinner?"

Her short shapely legs peeked out from under the hem of the dark green shirt. She wiggled from side to side, giving him a tantalizing glimpse of her hips.

"Nice wives don't torture their husbands."

"As you'd already pointed out, I believe I prefer adventurous to nice."

His gaze narrowed. "Don't toy with a hungry man, woman. Toss me those sweats."

"The honeymoon's over." She sighed dramatically and tugged on his oversize T-shirt. Then she picked up his navy blue sweatpants and crawled back on the bed to deliver them personally. Dropping them on his stomach, she sat back on her heels and grinned at him. "I *do* love you, Jake Parrish."

The silence following that statement stretched out for what seemed hours.

What could he say that wouldn't make him sound like the bastard he knew he was? So he said nothing, taking the familiar route of hiding from something that cut too close to home. Sitting up, he pulled the sweatpants on, then stood and walked to his dresser for a shirt. Anything to keep from gazing into her eyes and what was surely a stricken look.

"I guess the honeymoon really *is* over," she said finally, and scooted to the edge of the bed.

Jake inhaled deeply, shoved his arms into the sleeves of a plain white T-shirt, then pulled it on. When he had no other choice, he turned to look at her.

"Casey—"

"Don't." She held up one hand toward him and shook her head.

"Don't what?"

"Don't tell me about how this is a different sort of marriage and love wasn't a part of the bargain."

"Well, was it?"

"For me, yes." She pushed herself off the bed and took a step toward the door. Then she stopped and looked at him again. Jake felt her gaze slice into him and knew he deserved it. "Fine. You don't—or *won't*—love me."

"It's not you," he argued. He didn't want to hurt her, so he gave her as much of the truth as he was able. "It's me. I don't think I'm capable of love any-more."

"That's bull, Jake."

"What?" Surprised, he stared at her and even from across the room, saw the flash of anger that glittered in her eyes.

"You heard me."

"Casey—"

"No. What we just experienced together was—"

"Lust," he finished for her. "Pure and simple."

"Is that all you felt? Really?"

His gaze dropped a fraction and Casey saw it. She knew he had felt a hell of a lot more than lust. It was in his touch. In his kiss. In his every embrace. He loved her. But he was too damned stubborn to admit it.

"There's no reason we can't be happy in this marriage, Casey. We can be husband and wife. Enjoy each other. Raise our children and have as good a marriage, if not better, than most people have."

She nodded and waited for him to finish.

He took a deep breath and said, "Don't ask for what I can't give you, Casey. It will only hurt both of us."

Amazing. Did he actually *believe* that garbage?

Facing him, she crossed her arms over her chest and tilted her head to one side to stare at him.

"You're wrong, Jake."

He blinked and defensively folded his own arms across his chest.

"You don't want me to expect love from you? All right, I won't. But that's *your* loss, Jake. Not mine."

He lifted his chin as if expecting a blow, and she delivered it with her next words.

"I *do* love you, you big idiot. But as of right now, I'm through saying it."

"What's that supposed to mean?"

"It means that you can go ahead and pretend anything you like. But you *love* me, Jake Parrish. I know it." She crossed the room to him in several angry strides, not stopping until she was directly in front of him.

Poking his chest with her index finger to underline each word, she went on, "We'll be husband and wife. We'll enjoy each other. Raise our children. But until you can admit that you love me, we'll have only *half* a marriage."

"Casey—"

"And you'll have to be the first one to say it, Jake. I won't tell you again that I love you. Not until you've said it to me."

He shook his head slightly, and she wanted to kick him.

"You will say it, Jake. You will, or you'll be cheating yourself—and *me* out of something precious few people ever feel."

He reached for her, but she jumped back.

"Casey, can't you see that I'm only trying to protect both of us?"

"No. All I see is a man too hardheaded for his own good."

His jaw tightened and his gaze narrowed.

Casey nodded abruptly and turned her back on him. Headed for the doorway, she called over her shoulder, "Now come and have dinner, Jake. You'll need your strength."

"My strength," he repeated.

"Sure." She stopped, half turned and smiled at him. "I'm not going to cheat myself out of loving you or making love with you just because you're too stubborn to see what's right in front of you." Then she was gone, leaving him alone in the half-light.

"Casey…" She really was going to act as though nothing was wrong. She was going to go on and have a marriage whether he helped or not. He felt like an idiot.

He stared after her for a long moment and tried to figure out what had gone wrong with his perfectly reasonable plan.

A week later he was still trying.

One hairy lopsided ear slapped his cheek, and just to add insult to injury, Stumbles turned and barked in his face.

"All right," Jake muttered, pushing the dog off his lap and onto the passenger seat. "Look out your own window for a while."

Obligingly Stumbles rose on his hind legs, curled his front paws over the lowered window glass and leaned his head out into the forty-mile-an-hour wind.

Jake scowled at the mutt, then swung his gaze back to stare blankly out the windshield. There had been no snow all week, and the sun had turned the earlier snowfalls into slushy mud. Everything was brown. Which matched his mood. He'd driven this same lonely stretch of road so many times he could have done it blindfolded. Even in the muck. Since no concentration was necessary, his mind began to wander. Naturally it wandered straight to Casey.

A whole week and she had been as good as her word. Not one more peep out of her about love and forever. They made love, spent their days and their evenings together. He helped her with her growing list of catering clients and gratefully accepted her assistance with the ranch books. They talked about the baby and Christmas, played with Stumbles and planned a nursery. Just yesterday they'd gone out and chopped down a tall Scotch pine and dragged it back to the house to be decorated. They ate together, slept together and did everything any other married couple did.

He grumbled, shifted in the seat and slammed his palm against the steering wheel.

Stumbles whined.

"Sorry," he said, then laughed at himself for apologizing to a dog.

Dammit, he was getting exactly what he'd insisted he'd wanted. Why wasn't he happy?

Because he missed hearing those three little words from her.

He missed seeing the words in her eyes.

"Hell." He glanced at the dog. "She even tells *you* she loves you."

Stumbles whined again, stretched out on the seat and laid his head on his master's thigh.

"Yeah, I know. I love you, too." Jake reached down and scratched behind the dog's ears. Stumbles scooted closer.

"Strange, don't you think? I can say those words to you. But not to her."

In the distance a large dark brown van pulled out of the ranch drive and started down the road toward Jake, obviously headed back to town.

He squinted into the afternoon sunshine and fought a growing tide of unease rising inside him. The closer he got to that damned van, the worse he felt. When they were separated by no more than ten feet, Jake pulled to one side and stopped to let the vehicle pass.

Long after the driver's friendly wave, he still sat there. Engine idling, dog climbing over him, he simply stared through the windshield at the house.

It had started again.

"Yes, I know, Mother," Casey was saying as he stomped into the kitchen. "I only thought you'd want to know. I never expected you to *do* anything."

He glanced at her. She smiled, but he didn't return it. He couldn't. Not now. Not when everything he'd feared would happen had only just begun.

"I'm sure Father is more than ready to go," Casey said, and rolled her eyes at Jake. "Yes, Paris is probably very pretty right now."

Paris.

Casey held up her index finger as if telling him she would only be another minute or two.

"Mother, I realize you're not the grandmother type. No one *expects* you to bake cookies or change diapers."

God forbid.

"I know, Mother. Yes, I'm sure Jake will understand that a pregnant woman is bound to gain weight and be unsightly.''

Apparently talking to her mother on the telephone was no more pleasant than talking to her in person. But he didn't want to feel sorry for Casey now. No, right now, he wanted to ride the growing wave of anger and disappointment threatening to choke off his air. He wanted to surround himself with it and tell himself that he had been right to be wary. That he had *known* nothing would come of this marriage.

Hurrying through the kitchen, he glanced into the great room, absently noted the still-bare Christmas tree in front of the tall windows, then went on down the hall. He knew where the packages would be. The master bedroom. Where else?

Whenever the UPS man had delivered Linda's never-ending chain of parcels, they'd been piled on the bed so his devoted wife could amuse herself in comfort. Well, he wasn't going to stand by and let it happen all over again. Linda had damn near ruined him with her wild spending and extravagant indulgences. She'd been the only woman he'd ever known who'd actually seemed to *require* a dozen new pairs of shoes every six weeks.

He rounded the corner and spied them immediately—a relatively small stack of packages piled on a chair near the door. Snatching the top one, he ripped off the brown paper, pulled back the lid and stared down at the result of Casey's first foray into spending.

A flannel shirt.

For *him*.

Frowning, Jake quickly went through the rest of the packages, ripping the paper free and tossing it onto the floor. Flannel shirts. Socks. Two pairs of jeans and a rain slicker.

All for him.

Not only that, they were exactly what he would have bought for himself if he'd ever had the time or inclination to shop.

He dropped the last package and shoved one hand through his hair. Confused, he tried to figure out what this might mean. What it did to his theories.

"Well," Casey said dryly from behind him, "I can hardly wait to watch you on Christmas morning."

He turned around to look at her.

She smiled and shook her head at the mess littering the floor. "It's a good thing I didn't have your Christmas present delivered. You're worse than a kid."

"These are all for me," he finally said.

"Is that a problem?" she asked, stepping into the room and picking up a sheet of torn paper from the rug.

"No," he said. Not a problem. *Mystery* was a better word. "But why? When did you get these?"

"At Annie's shop. She had a great catalog there." Both eyebrows lifted. "Don't tell her, but I swiped it. I didn't think you'd mind, Jake. Your jeans are disintegrating. You stay more wet than dry in your ratty old rain slicker, and I'm afraid Stumbles has developed a taste for your socks."

She'd noticed. She'd shopped for him. Scowling

slightly, he bent to pick up the rest of the paper he had tossed about in his frenzy. When he straightened, she looked at him closely.

"My buying clothes for you really surprised you, didn't it?"

"Yeah." He snorted. "You could say that."

"Jeez, Jake, I'm your wife." She shrugged and reached up to plant a quick kiss on his cheek. "I—" Clamping her lips together tightly, she shook her head.

She'd almost said it.

Strange that words *not* said could hurt so much.

"I'm glad you're back," she said in an obvious change of subject. "I'd like to decorate the tree tonight."

"Uh-huh," he answered absently, his brain still adjusting to a woman shopping for him, not herself.

"I was wondering," she went on, speaking a little more loudly to get his attention. "The lights have to go on first. Do you want to do it or would you rather I did?"

"Lights?" he repeated, an image of the tall pine coming to mind. "I'll do it. You'd have to use a ladder, and you might fall."

She nodded. "All right, thanks. Oh, I found an old box of Christmas ornaments in the garage today, so I brought them inside. Hope that's okay."

Now he was really confused. "But I showed you where all the new stuff was yesterday." Every imported glass ball and color-coordinated decoration had cost him a bundle. Naturally Linda hadn't settled for anything but the best.

"Yeah," Casey said slowly, "but it was all so...I don't know. Anyway, I decided to look around for the things I remembered your mother setting out each year."

"Why?" he had to ask.

"OK, Jake," she said, sighing. "The things you showed me yesterday are pretty...but they remind me too much of the professionally decorated trees my mother gets done every year." She shrugged. "For our first Christmas I wanted everything to be..."

"Perfect?"

"Homey," she corrected. "You don't mind if I use your mother's things, do you?"

"No," he said quickly. Of course he didn't mind. He just wasn't sure he understood.

"Good." Casey smiled and turned for the door. "Wash up for dinner, then we'll get this Christmas on the road!"

Christmas, he thought as he sat down on the mattress. Christmas with his mother's decorations, a real tree and Casey.

He should be happy.

Dammit, why wouldn't he let himself be happy?

Eleven

The next morning bright and early Casey stood in the great room saying goodbye to Jake.

"You'll stay off the ladder?" he asked pointedly.

She chuckled and held up her right hand. "Promise. Besides, I don't need the ladder now." She glanced up at the newly placed strings of lights encircling the floor-to-ceiling front windows. Cheerful Christmas colors shone in the gleaming windowpanes. "Pretty, aren't they?"

"Beautiful," he said softly.

Casey turned to find him staring—not at the lights he'd insisted on hanging himself—but at her. A slow tide of pleasure washed through her. He loved her. She could see it in his eyes whenever he looked at her. Why couldn't he see it, too? Why couldn't he admit to the truth?

"You sure you want to take your car to town?" he asked abruptly. "I could leave the Jeep with you. One of your brothers can drive to the lake."

Casey shook her head. What was this husband of hers going to be like when her pregnancy was further along? He worried about everything, watched her diet like a hawk and *still* couldn't see that he loved her. "You go ahead," she said. "Since you put the snow tires on my car, it's fine. And so am I."

He nodded and grabbed his fishing pole. "I'll be back before dark."

"I'll be here."

He looked at her for a long moment, then bent down to kiss her. What he'd meant to be a brief dusting of lips, Casey instinctively deepened, drawing him closer by looping her arms around his neck.

A low groan eased from the back of his throat, and he dropped the fishing pole to squeeze her tightly. No matter what else lay between them, they shared an incredible magic every time they touched. When she was sure she had his complete attention, she broke the kiss and took a step back. Judging by the tortured expression on his face, her work was done. She might have pretended to go along with his ridiculous notions of what their marriage should be like. But she had never promised to make it easy for him.

"Have fun," she said. "Say hi to Nathan and J.T."

Jake inhaled sharply, narrowed his gaze and jerked her a nod. "I don't have to go fishing, you know."

Though it felt wonderful just knowing he'd be willing to give up a fishing trip with her brothers in favor of being with her, Casey shooed him out of the kitchen. "Yes, you do. The three of you have been talking about going ice fishing since the wedding."

Resigned, he picked up his pole and tackle box and headed for the door. "It seemed like a good idea at the time," he conceded.

"How carving a hole in the ice and sitting all day huddled beside it waiting for a fish to swim by can seem like a good idea at *any* time is beyond me." She smiled, then reached up to tug the collar of his coat higher around his neck.

"You're a girl," he said, wiggling his eyebrows. "Girls don't understand guy stuff."

Maybe not, she thought. But girls understand enough to take advantage when their men were off doing guy stuff. While Jake was busy with her brothers, Casey planned to talk to Annie. She had finally come to the conclusion that, to fight Jake's memories of his ex-wife, she had to know what exactly she was up against.

Dawn was just beginning to creep across the sky, dragging soft rose-colored clouds into the growing brightness. It would be at least another couple of hours before she could call Annie.

She stood at the front window waving until Jake drove out of the yard, then she headed for the warmth of the fireplace. Sitting down with a cup of hot cocoa, she stared into the flames and made her plans.

"She spent nearly every dime the man ever made," Annie said, and reached for another fresh-baked cinnamon roll. "These are really good, Case.

But you didn't have to bribe me to make me talk, you know.''

"Don't think of it as a bribe. Think of it as an incentive.''

Annie arched one black eyebrow and inclined her head. "That *is* easier on my gentle sensibilities.''

Incentive, bribe, but what the cinnamon rolls really were, were the products of restless hands and a too-busy brain. Those two hours between dawn and the more respectable 8 a.m. took an alarmingly long time to pass.

"So,'' Casey said, and reached for Annie's coffeepot, "the reason Jake divorced Linda was that she spent all his money?'' that would certainly explain his behavior the day the UPS man made a delivery at the ranch.

"That was part of it, sure. But that wasn't what finally ended it.''

Casey glanced over her shoulder toward the living room. She certainly didn't want Lisa wandering in to overhear her mother and aunt discussing her uncle. The muted sounds of an early-morning children's television show drifted to her, along with Lisa's occasional giggle. Stumbles and the little girl had formed an immediate kinship, probably because Lisa believed in sharing her cinnamon roll with the ever-hungry dog.

Turning back to her friend, Casey poured her some more coffee, inhaling the scent wistfully and said, "Tell me.''

"First you have to understand, Jake really thought he loved the woman.''

Silly that those words could sting. Of course he'd believed he was in love. He'd married the woman, after all. Casey smiled to herself. That didn't prove a thing. He'd married her, too. And seemed determined to prove that he *didn't* love her.

"Frankly," Annie went on, licking icing from her fingertip, "I never did understand what he saw in the woman. She had mean eyes."

Casey grinned and patted her friend's arm. "Thanks. Now, what happened?"

"Simple enough." Annie picked up her coffee cup with both hands. Squeezing the Star Trek memorial mug tightly, she muttered, "He came home early one afternoon and found dear Linda in bed with a BMW salesman from Reno."

"What?"

"Yep." Annie's lips thinned angrily at the memory. "He stood outside his own bedroom door and listened to his wife tell her lover that he shouldn't be worried about her husband finding out. She said Jake was such an idiot for love. He'd forgive her anything."

Good Lord. Emotions raced through Casey, each of them demanding to be recognized. Anger, primarily. At Linda for hurting Jake so. But sympathy for Jake, who'd been so deeply wounded, quickly took precedence.

No wonder he didn't want to talk about love. No wonder he couldn't bring himself to care openly for her. He'd tried it once and had his heart handed back to him in pieces.

"Yeah, it was really ugly for a while," Annie said,

and Casey's gaze shot up to meet hers. "But you know, I finally figured out that he couldn't really have loved that bitch."

"What do you mean?"

"He was more furious than hurt. Oh, no doubt, he considers himself lanced to the core." Annie nodded. "Most men tend to attribute gallons more blood than necessary to any wound, no matter how slight."

"Slight?" Casey felt as though she should leap up and defend her husband's right to bleed.

"I'm not saying he wasn't hurt," Annie went on. "Only that it was more like he was embarrassed. For letting himself be such a fool for the wrong woman."

Propping one elbow on the table and cupping her hand in her chin, Casey muttered thoughtfully, "So now he won't be a fool for *any* woman."

"Hey, he'll come around." Annie shrugged. "Eventually."

"I'm not so sure." Casey straightened, reached for a second cinnamon roll and broke it apart before laying it down on her plate. "And why should he?"

"Huh?"

"Well, look at it from his side. He's got a wife. A baby on the way. He knows I love him, but doesn't want to hear about it. He's determined we will have a nice civilized marriage without any of the bother of love."

"Ooh." Annie shuddered. "Sounds cozy."

"Yeah, and I've been going along with it."

"Are you nuts?"

"Mommy," Lisa called from the living room, "I hafta go potty again."

"You go on then, honey. I'll be there in a minute."

"No, I'm not nuts," Casey said, and took a bite of the pastry. She chewed quickly, swallowed and said, "Not anymore, anyway. Dammit, Annie, I've *seen* a civilized marriage. Up close and personal."

Her friend winced in sympathy, and Casey looked away. She knew Annie understood. She'd visited often enough during their growing-up years to see the cool tension between Henderson and Hilary Oakes. Casey's parents had had a so-called successful marriage based on wealth, a love of travel and a closed eye to indiscretions.

But she, Casey, had always dreamed of more. Those dreams had comforted her through long lonely nights and fed her fantasies for years. Most of those fantasies, at least since the time she was fifteen, she admitted silently, had revolved around Jake.

Now she had the chance to make her dreams come true. All she had to do was somehow convince Jake that she really did love him. And that it was safe for him to love her.

"Mommy." Lisa's voice sounded muffled, faraway. "I'm done."

Casey grinned. How did a child manage to put three syllables into a word like "done"?

Annie sighed and stood up. "Get used to the sound of that," she said with a short laugh. "It'll be your turn soon enough."

Alone at the table, Casey sat back in her chair and glanced at the local newspaper. The front-page headline of the *Simpson Salutation* read: HARRY BIGGS

WINS CHURCH RAFFLE. And in smaller type, just beneath it: WIFE STUNNED.

She chuckled and picked up the newspaper to read about Harry Biggs's prize. Apparently just about anything could make headlines in a small-town daily.

A smile eased up Casey's features as she stared blankly at the pages in her hand.

She had an idea.

Three days later what she hoped would be the answer to her marital problems lay unopened on the kitchen table. She glanced at the neatly folded newspaper and smiled. It would work, she told herself.

It had to work.

Turning her mind back to the business at hand, she looked down at the pan on the stove and started stirring the contents. Boiling frantically, the mixture of lemon juice and granulated sugar frothed up the sides of the pan. She whisked the bubbles into submission again and again, then scowled when someone knocked on the front door.

Glancing at Stumbles, her fearless protector, Casey laughed. The dog, sound asleep under the kitchen table, hadn't even flinched at the sound.

She glanced down at the filling for her lemon-meringue pie and grimaced. If she took it off the fire now, it would be ruined. If she left it to go answer the door, it would boil over and the kitchen would be a sea of lemony sugar.

Hoping against hope a serial killer wouldn't be so polite as to knock on the door, she hollered, "Come in!"

Keeping the whisk moving rapidly through the frothy mixture, she locked her gaze on the entryway, waiting.

"Casey?"

A deep voice. One she hadn't heard in quite a while. One she'd expected to hear say, "I do," not so very long ago.

Steven.

"Casey?" he called again. "Where are you?"

She cleared her throat, swallowed, then said, "In here."

He stepped into her line of vision through the kitchen doorway and stopped. His gaze shot to hers, and for a long moment, neither of them spoke. Finally he broke the silence.

"Can I come in?"

"You're in already." Taking a deep breath, she told herself there was no point in being nasty. Besides, if she was honest about the whole thing, she was grateful he'd jilted her. If he hadn't taken off for Mexico, she might not have found her way back to Jake. In that spirit she smiled and nodded. "Come on in, Steven."

He seemed to relax then and crossed the main room tugging a muffler from his neck and opening his overcoat as he moved to join her in the kitchen. He looked good. Tanned from his escape to Mexico, his skin was the color of polished brass. Neither as big nor as handsome as Jake, Steven Miller still managed to make female hearts flutter.

Soft brown hair waved back from a high forehead, and his dark brown eyes watched her warily. Dressed in a black overcoat, steel gray suit with a white shirt and a boldly striped red power tie, he looked completely out of place in the homey kitchen, and just as uneasy.

"Oh, relax," she said. She couldn't stand to see him waiting for a blow that wasn't coming. "I'm not going to hit you."

"Not that I'd blame you any," he said with a wry grin. "But I appreciate your restraint."

"What are you doing here, Steven?" And why today? The day she wanted to gather her thoughts for a confrontation with Jake.

"When I got back from Mexico, my mother told me where to find you."

"That's *how* you got here. Not why."

"Right." He ducked his head, peeked into the pan she was still stirring, then straightened and paced the length of the room. He stopped by the fogged-over kitchen windows. When there was a good ten feet separating them, he went on, "I guess I just had to see for myself that you were all right."

"I am now," she said. "I wasn't when I got your note."

He winced and stooped to pet Stumbles, the traitor, who was busy slobbering all over Steven's snow-dusted Gucci loafers. "I *am* sorry about that, Casey."

"That's something, I suppose." She whipped the lemony foam a little more quickly, surprised there was still a small corner of her that was angry at him for what he'd done.

"Look, I tried to talk to you the night before the wedding."

"What?"

"I called your parents' house. Talked to your father." He straightened again, frowning at the slobber on his tassles. "I told him I had to talk to you, but he kept insisting you were not to be disturbed."

Her father? But he hadn't told *her* Steven had called.

"He didn't tell you, did he?"

"That you called? No." She shook her head, denying the cold unsettling feeling creeping into her chest. For some reason, she knew she wasn't going to like whatever else it was he'd come to say.

"Not just that," Steven said softly. "He didn't tell you I wouldn't be at the church."

Her world rocked a bit. Her fingers tightened on the handle of the pan. The knot in her chest tightened until it threatened to choke off her air. Her own father had known her groom wasn't going to put in an appearance at the church. Why hadn't he said anything? Why had he allowed her to go through with it? To be humiliated in front of hundreds of people. She wanted to ask all those questions aloud. She wanted to demand answers to everything. But all she could manage was, "He *knew?*"

"Yeah, he knew. I told him I couldn't go through with it." Steven pushed one hand through his hair, and Casey absently noted that it fell right back into place. "I also told him I didn't think *you* wanted to get married, either." He glanced around the kitchen and smiled sheepishly. "At least, not to me."

"I didn't," she said, and was surprised that her voice worked.

Steven rushed on, barely nodding to acknowledge her statement. "You know your father. He just brushed it all off. Said it was last-minute jitters and I should just show up on time and the marriage would take care of itself." Steven glanced at her and she saw real regret and shame on his features. "I really thought he would tell you, Casey. I never expected you to be there at the church. Waiting."

It sounded like her father, all right. Of course he wouldn't have believed Steven. He never would have believed that someone from their social circle would ruin a carefully arranged and planned wedding. How like Henderson Oakes not to even mention to his daughter the possibility of being jilted.

She felt color rise in her cheeks. "But you were there. You left a note for me."

"Yeah. I drove past the church and saw all the cars. Then I knew that he hadn't said anything." Her ex-fiancé took a few steps closer and stopped. "So I pulled into the parking lot long enough to slip a note to one of my ushers."

"You couldn't come and see me personally?"

"I should have."

"Yeah," she agreed, and turned the fire off. Carrying the pan to the counter where the pie crust was ready and waiting, she poured the mixture in and said, "But I almost understand why you didn't." She got cold chills just thinking about how her parents and his would have reacted to an in-person announcement.

It had been bad enough watching the Oakeses and Millers glaring at each other, each couple blaming the other for the disaster that was their children. If Steven had actually been there, the shouting and the humiliation would have been twice as difficult to bear.

"So," he said, glancing around the house, "are you happy? Mom told me you got married."

"And pregnant."

Two light brown eyebrows lifted.

"I'm *very* happy, Steven," she said. "Actually I ought to thank you. I won't," she added, "but I should."

"I'm glad, Casey." He laughed to fill an awkward silence. "Relieved, too."

She walked up to him and gave him a hug. "You're forgiven, Steven. Relax."

He nodded, then locking his arms around her waist, lifted her off the floor and squeezed her gently. "He's a lucky guy," he said with a chuckle.

Steven's laughter choked off when the back door flew open and crashed against the kitchen wall.

"Damn right," Jake said.

Twelve

Casey's feet hit the floor jarringly enough to rattle her teeth. She looked up at Jake and realized she'd never seen him so angry. Splotches of red, caused not entirely by the cold, stained his cheeks, and his eyes flashed as he looked from Steven to her and back again.

"Goddammit, get your hands off my wife!" Blind with pain, Jake felt like throwing his head back and howling with the rage boiling through him.

"It's not what you think," the man said.

"Calm down, Jake." Casey faced him, meeting his gaze squarely. "You're acting like a nut." Hurriedly she closed the kitchen door to shut out the frigid air.

She was criticizing *his* behavior?

The other man spoke again. "Look. Maybe I'd

better just introduce myself and we can start over.''
He extended his right hand. ''My name's Steven Miller.''

Steven.

Jake shot a look at Casey and read her expression
easily enough. Glancing back at the expensively
dressed man, he gave himself over to the pulse-
pounding anger throbbing within. He had never before really known what it meant when people said
they were so angry they ''saw red.'' Until now. It
wasn't bad enough that he had *again* walked into his
own house and found his wife in the arms of another
man. No, this time, it had to be *the* other man. The
man she had intended to marry.

Pain, white-hot and insistent, shimmered inside
him. Before he knew what he was doing, he took a
single step forward, batted the man's hand out of his
way and slammed his fist into his jaw.

Jake felt the satisfying thud all the way up his arm.
He watched with grim vindication as the intruder
staggered backward into the table. The man's fall
knocked an unfinished lemon pie to the floor, crust
and filling splashed across the tiles. Stumbles shot
out from under the table and rushed for the fallen
goodies. The man wobbled unsteadily and dropped
to the floor, one hand clapped to his jaw.

It was only then that Jake turned to look at his
wife again. His heart hammered in his chest. His
brain raced. His blood was still boiling. Despite his
fears, he'd never really expected Casey to cheat on
him. Nor had he expected the depth of pain betrayal
would bring.

What he had lived through at Linda's hands seemed insignificant in comparison. This pain stabbed at him. Slashed at him. Every moment that passed only made the ache worse.

"Are you out of your mind?" Casey shouted.

"What?" His breathing labored, he stared at her. What did *she* have to be angry about?

Bending down, she helped the other man to his feet. It didn't make Jake feel any better to notice that the guy carefully kept his distance from Casey once he was standing.

"Why did you hit him?" she demanded.

"Why was he holding *my* wife?"

"It was a hug, Jake. Just a hug." She waved one hand at the mess on the floor being slurped up by a happy dog. "I was baking a pie, Jake. This is the kitchen, for God's sake. Not the bedroom."

He lifted one black eyebrow, silently demanding that she remember the time he and she had used the kitchen as a trysting place.

She flushed, and he knew the memory had come to her.

"I know what I saw, Casey." Why couldn't she understand what it had felt like to see her in someone else's arms?

"You saw what you've been expecting to see." She lifted her chin and looked him dead in the eye. "You've been waiting for something like this since the day we got married."

"What?" Had she known all along what was going through his mind?

"You didn't think I knew, did you?"

He sighed. "Annie."

"Yes, Annie. Your *sister* told me everything that *you* should have told me."

His chest tightened. He hadn't wanted her to know. Hadn't wanted Casey to know that his ex-wife had thought so little of him that she had flaunted her lovers in his own house. Jesus, what kind of thing was that for a man to know about himself? Did she really think he would want to tell *her?*

"There was no reason for you to know about Linda. It had nothing to do with us." He folded his arms across his chest in an unconscious but useless attempt to hold his heart in place.

"Nothing to do with us?" Casey moved forward then stopped again.

"Excuse me," Steven said from his position behind her. "Perhaps I should be leaving."

"Shut up," Jake said.

"Shut up," Casey snapped at the same time.

Steven shrugged and turned to watch the gorging dog.

"How can you say what happened with Linda has nothing to do with us?" Casey demanded.

"It happened a long time ago," Jake said.

"And what happened then has colored everything that has passed between us."

"Casey—"

"No, let's get it said. Finally let's get it said."

Jake flinched away from the sheen of tears he saw sparkling in her eyes. His entire body ached with the urge to run from the room. To put the pain aside. To forget seeing Casey in Steven's arms and just go back to the way things had been between them.

In a last-ditch attempt to postpone the inevitable, he said as much. "Stop, Casey. Stop now. We can forget all about what happened today."

Steven snorted.

They ignored him.

"We can go back to the way we were," Jake went on. "It was all right, wasn't it?"

"'All right' isn't good enough, Jake," she said quietly. "Not anymore. I want to be loved. I want a *real* marriage. And in real marriages, people talk to each other. Trust each other." Her bottom lip quivered a bit, but she charged ahead. "For weeks you've been watching, waiting for me to do something that would prove to you I was just like Linda. You've been holding your breath, almost hoping for the chance to say, 'See? I knew I shouldn't love you.' Instead of realizing I am *nothing* like Linda, instead of snatching at our chance for happiness, you chose to sit back and throw stones at everything we had."

"I never said you were like Linda."

She sucked in a breath and let her gaze slide over him slowly before looking into his eyes again. Disappointment filled her, and Casey shook her head slowly. "You didn't have to say it. It was there. Between us. Every day." She snatched her purse from the counter, then reached back and grabbed hold of Steven's jacket. Tugging her ex-fiancé toward the door, she told her husband, "Fine, then, Jake. If you think what you saw is enough reason to throw away my love, great. You win. Now you don't have to put up with me."

"Where are you going?" Jake moved closer.

"Why do you care?" She shoved Steven through the open door, grabbed her coat and glared at the man she loved. "I don't understand how I could be so in love with a man as impossibly arrogant and stupid and pigheaded as you, Jake Parrish!" Walking into the mudroom, she snapped, "But if I try *really* hard, maybe I'll get over it."

Then she was gone and his only company was a delighted dog and the echo of the door slamming shut.

"Where are we?"

Casey blinked and looked at Steven. "What did you say?"

He worked his jaw back and forth, then said again, "Where are we?"

She glanced at the building directly in front of them. Holiday paintings decorated the windows of Annie's beauty shop. She almost sneered at Santa and his happy elves. Strange, she didn't even remember heading for Annie's place. But then, she hardly remembered the drive into town, either. So angry at Jake she could hardly speak, she had simply demanded Steven's keys, climbed into the driver's seat of his Porsche and taken off with Steven in the passenger seat.

Vaguely she recalled hearing her ex-fiancé groan when she occasionally failed to engage the clutch of his precious car, but she'd ignored him. Every ounce of her being was too filled with images of her husband for her to think of anything else.

Of all the hardheaded, insulting, chest-pounding Neanderthals she'd ever known, Jake Parrish took the prize.

Imagine that fool actually believing that she would cheat on him! Oh, she understood about Linda. Fine, the woman had been a treacherous bitch. But for him to tar her with the same brush was unforgivable.

"Casey," Steven said, "do you know a good doctor in town? I really think I ought to have my jaw looked at."

She glared at him briefly. "You're talking, Steven. It's not broken."

"I don't know." He held one hand to his cheek and worked his jaw again. "I hear it popping when I do this."

"Then don't do that." Grumbling under her breath, Casey opened the car door and got out, slamming the door behind her.

She didn't wait for him to follow her. Instead, she stomped through the few feet of slush to the beauty parlor and went inside.

The silence was deafening.

Jake rolled his shoulders, glanced at the dog and scowled. "What are *you* smiling about?"

Stumbles ducked his head and scuttled out of the room.

Disgusted with himself and the whole situation, Jake started pacing, his boots clicking angrily against the tiles.

"What did she expect me to think?" he demanded of no one. "I come in the door to my own house and find her with another man and I'm not supposed to be mad?"

His words echoed back at him and he flinched at the loneliness of the sound. He came to a sudden stop and looked down at the now shiny-clean pie plate. Stumbles had eaten every last crumb.

Lemon meringue.

Jake's favorite.

She'd been making his favorite pie. From scratch. For him.

His gaze shifted to the table where the day's paper lay alongside an opened Christmas catalog and a list of gifts to buy for Lisa, Annie, his aunt and uncle, and his father.

Casey had been thinking about him. She was always thinking about him.

"Then *I* walk in the door and start acting like some deranged actor in a third-rate play." He slumped against the cooking island and let his mind drift back over the past several weeks.

Laughter had filled the house. There was a warmth to the place that hadn't been there since he was a child. Even now the scent of the Christmas tree wafted to him, making him feel the season as he hadn't in a very long time. Every time he walked through the door, he felt the welcome in the air. Felt Casey's love.

For weeks he'd been surrounded by that love. Somehow he'd been given a second chance at happiness. That too-young girl he'd wanted so badly five years before had come back into his life and given him everything he'd ever dreamed of.

And he'd allowed his fear of losing that happiness to ensure that he did.

Of course she wasn't like Linda. On some gut level, he'd always known that. It was only his pride that had kept him from acknowledging it until now, when it was too late. Had she left him for good? Was she so disgusted with him she was never coming back? And could he live without her?

No.

He couldn't.

"So, what are you going to do?" he muttered, and braced both hands on the cooking island behind him. His mind filled with images of Casey and chocolate éclairs and long slow deep kisses.

His imagination drew mental pictures of Casey— in a few more months her belly round and heavy with their child. Her warm smile and the gleam in her eyes as she looked at him.

Abruptly he pushed away from the counter and raced outside. There was only one thing he *could* do. Get her back. Where she belonged.

With him.

"Casey!" Annie called out a welcome as the door flew open. "I was going to call you in a few minutes. I just saw the newspaper."

Casey cringed and glanced around the tiny shop, dismayed to find one customer in the chair and two other women on the sofa waiting their turns.

She didn't want to talk about the ad she'd taken

out in the local paper. Not now. Not when everything had changed so drastically. Dammit, she'd had such high hopes that the ad in the paper would convince Jake to take a chance on their happiness.

"What's wrong?" Annie asked, and walked toward her friend and sister-in-law, customers forgotten.

"What *isn't* wrong?" Casey muttered. "That would take far less time."

"Oh, no. What did Jake do now?"

The front door opened again and Annie's gaze shifted to the newcomer.

"Annie," Casey said on a sigh. "Meet Steven."

"Steven? *The* Steven?"

"Why did that sound like '*The* Jack the Ripper'?" Steven asked.

"Sorry. Jeez," Annie winced in sympathy "—what happened to you? Your cheek is purple." Her gaze shot to Casey. "Jake?"

"Jake."

"I don't mean to be a bother," Steven interrupted. "But could I have some ice, do you think?"

"Sure. Get it yourself." Annie jerked her head toward the back room.

Steven's eyebrows lifted, but he went.

Annie turned to Casey. "What's going on?"

"Annie, I don't even know. Jake came in the house, found me hugging Steven and slugged him."

"Oh, boy."

Rushed whispers erupted from the corner waiting area, and Casey glanced at the two middle-aged women. Immediately the pair straightened up and pretended an air of casual disinterest. The customer in Annie's chair didn't bother to pretend. She had her neck craned back so far to listen that Casey was surprised her head didn't snap off.

Too bad for Jake, she thought. He hated gossip so much he really shouldn't go around hitting people.

Steven came back into the room just then, a sandwich bag full of ice held to his jaw. His interested gaze swept over Annie slowly, appreciatively. When he met her steely blue eyes, he shrugged helplessly, then looked at Casey.

"Will you be all right here if I leave?"

"Running out on her again, eh?" Annie said.

He stiffened. "I didn't run out on her."

"Jilt's an ugly word."

The whispering started up in the corner again, and Casey sighed. She was going to be the subject of Simpson gossip for months. If not years. Decades from now, her grandchildren would be hearing the story of the day their grandma's old boyfriend had come to town and how their granddaddy had cleaned his clock.

"Of course she'll be all right," Annie snapped. "Why wouldn't she be?"

"I didn't mean to imply anything."

Casey looked away from them. She didn't have the energy to referee. She stared through the window at Main Street, hardly noticing the brightly colored plastic candy canes that hung from the lampposts or the evergreen swags stretched across the narrow drive. Casey sighed tiredly and felt what little strength she had left disappear as Jake drove up. She frowned when he parked the Jeep directly behind Steven's car, blocking it from moving.

"Hey, Jake," Mr. Holbrook at the hardware store said. "Congratulations."

Jake smiled, nodded and wondered what the hell the man was talking about.

"I think it's just so sweet!" This from an older female voice. Jake turned to see Dolly Fenwick grinning at him from the sidewalk. "And so romantic," she continued with a heavy sigh. "You tell Casey I said Merry Christmas."

He nodded. What was going on? Jake glanced at the car Casey had sped away in. Blocked by the Jeep, that Porsche wasn't going anywhere. At least not if Casey tried to leave in it.

Hurrying to the beauty shop, he opened the door and stepped into the most important fight of his life.

Steven dropped his ice bag, bent his knees and lifted both fists like an old-fashioned prizefighter. Bobbing and weaving, he prepared for battle.

Jake frowned at him. "I didn't come here for you," he said.

Steven's eyebrows lifted, but he slowly dropped his fists, still keeping a wary eye on Jake.

"Why *did* you come?" Casey asked tiredly.

"I came to get you."

"Why? Afraid I stole the family silver?"

There was a muffled snort from the cluster of chairs in the corner.

"Dammit, Casey!" He realized he was shouting so he lowered his voice. "I came to take you home."

"I'm not going home."

"Atta girl," somebody murmured.

"You're not leaving me." Amazing he was able to squeeze those words out past the tightness in his throat. He glanced around the little shop, from his sister's disgusted expression to Steven and to the older ladies watching him with open interest. He dismissed them all. He didn't care who heard him. He didn't care if people talked about him for weeks. All he knew was that he had to convince his wife to give him another chance. He only hoped he could figure out the right things to say. "I won't let you leave me, Casey."

"Leave *you?*" Surprise tinged her voice.

"Everything you said is true," Jake blurted, and stepped closer to her. "I was a jerk. I was standing back and trying not to care. But I cared, anyway."

"You did?" She cocked her head and watched him carefully.

"Of course I did." He closed the space between them, but didn't touch her. He couldn't risk that yet. If she moved away from him, it would hurt too much. "I loved you from the beginning, Casey."

"Say that again."

He smiled. "I love you. Always have. Please, Casey, don't leave me. Stumbles and I would never survive."

Her lips twitched. "A dirty trick, using Stumbles against me."

"I'm desperate."

"How desperate."

"Enough to try anything. Say anything. Casey, I

love you. Come home with me. Give me the chance to prove to you I can be foolishly lovesick as well as anybody.'' Risking it now, he placed both hands on her shoulders. "Don't leave me, Casey." He lowered his voice and bent his head so only she would hear him say, "If you leave, the loneliness and the pain will kill me."

"You big dummy."

He blinked and jerked his head back. "What?"

"You are such a dummy, Jake." She grinned at him and shook her head. "I wasn't going to leave you."

"You weren't?" The knot in his chest loosened, and breath came easily again to his straining lungs.

"Of course not." She reached up and smoothed one hand over his cheek. He turned his face into her touch. "I don't give up *that* easy," she said solemnly. "You're an aggravating man sometimes, Jake, but I love you."

He pulled in another breath.

"I don't *stop* loving you just because I'm angry. I only left the house because I needed to get away before I gave you the swift kick you deserved."

"From now on I give you permission to kick me whenever I need it."

"I'll remember that," she told him. Turning her head slightly, she looked at Annie. Her sister-in-law was grinning from ear to ear and wiping away a trickle of tears. "Hand me the newspaper, please."

Confused, Jake watched his sister grab the *Salutation* and slap it into Casey's waiting hand.

"If you read the paper in the morning like everybody else in town,'' Casey said, ''you would have seen this hours ago.'' Opening up the front page, she held it in front of her like a shield and waited for him to read it.

Jake's gaze swept the headline once, then again, just to assure himself he wasn't imagining things. But he wasn't. A smile spread slowly across his face. Now he understood what the people outside had been talking about. No doubt everyone in town would be discussing it for weeks.

But *this* kind of gossip he could grow to like.

He looked at the headline one last time and felt the last of his doubts and worries slip away. Right across the top of the page in bold black letters were the words: CASEY LOVES JAKE: A FOOL FOR LOVE.

He lifted his gaze to his wife's smiling face. Taking the newspaper from her, he tossed it to the floor and reached for her. He held her close to him and felt his world come right again.

With Casey in his arms, he had everything he would ever need. Looking down at her, he whispered, ''I guess being a fool for love can be a good thing.''

She nodded. ''If the fool you're in love with loves you right back.''

Then he kissed her, long and deep, and neither one of them heard the applause from the delighted onlookers.

Epilogue

Christmas afternoon…

"We really should get busy," Casey said, and snuggled closer. She and Jake were lying on the couch. "You know everyone will be here soon."

"No hurry," her husband muttered, holding her more tightly to his side.

She laughed and lifted her head to look down at him. "You've been saying that all day, Jake."

Of course, she wasn't complaining. Why would she? Spending Christmas day making love to a husband who adored her was a dream come true.

He smiled as he ran one fingertip across her jaw. "A man's entitled to spend his first Christmas with his new wife any way he chooses."

"Is that so?" One eyebrow arched high on her forehead.

He nodded. "It's a rule, I think."

Chuckling softly, she laid her head on his chest and stared at the Christmas tree, its lights blazing, its odd assortment of well-loved ornaments looking somehow…regal.

"It's a perfect Christmas, isn't it?" she whispered.

"Perfect," he repeated, and wrapped both arms around her. Outside, snow twisted in a cold wind and slapped against the windows. But inside, a fire burned, both in the hearth and between the two people lying so close on the sofa.

Beneath the Christmas tree a small mound of presents, wrapped in festive paper, lay waiting to be opened and appreciated. Close by, Stumbles snored gently, lost in dreams.

"Don't you want to open your present before your family gets here?" Casey asked as she listened to the steady beat of his heart beneath her ear.

"Nope," he said, stroking her back gently. "I've already got my presents."

She tipped her head back to look up at him and found him watching her through eyes that no longer hid his love. "You do?"

"I do. The only present I'll ever need is you. And the baby. And you."

She smiled. "You already said that."

"I want to say it. Over and over. As many times as you can stand to hear it." Cupping her cheek with one hand, he said, "I love you, Casey. More than I ever thought possible. Every day with you is magic. Every day is Christmas."

Tears stung her eyes, but she blinked them back

before raising herself high enough to kiss him gently. "I love you, too, Jake. Merry Christmas."

"Merry Christmas."

Then he kissed her, and when she closed her eyes, she could still see brightly colored lights twinkling merrily.

*   *   *   *   *